A MIDSUMMER NIGHT'S Dream

FAMILIUS

Published by Familius LLC, www.familius.com
Familius books are available at special discounts for bulk purchases
for sales promotions or for family or corporate use. Special
editions, including personalized covers, excerpts of existing books,
or books with corporate logos, can be created in large quantities
for special needs. For more information, contact Premium Sales at
559-876-2170 or email specialmarkets@familius.com.

Originally published by Sweet Cherry Publishing, Ltd, 2013
Text & illustration by Macaw Books, 2013

Library of Congress Catalog-in-Publication Data
2015942867
ISBN 9781942934271

Printed in the United States of America

Edited by Michele Robbins
Cover design by David Miles

10 9 8 7 6 5 4 3 2 1

First Edition

About
SHAKESPEARE

William Shakespeare, regarded as the greatest writer in the English language, was born in Stratford-upon-Avon in Warwickshire, England (around April 23, 1564). He was the third of eight children born to John and Mary Shakespeare.

Shakespeare was a poet, playwright, and dramatist. He is often known as England's national poet and the "Bard of Avon." Thirty-eight plays, 154 sonnets, two long narrative poems, and several other poems are attributed to him. Shakespeare's plays have been translated into every major language and are performed more often than those of any other playwright.

MAIN CHARACTERS

Hermia is young, strong-willed, and independent. She does not hesitate to go against her father's wishes, even in the face of death. She is in love with a nobleman named Lysander. She is also loved by Demetrius, another nobleman, but she does not return his love.

Lysander is a young nobleman in Athens. He is in love with Hermia, but Hermia's father does not want his daughter to marry him. When Hermia's life is in danger, Lysander persuades her to meet him in the woods, so they can run away and get married.

Demetrius is another nobleman. Egeus, Hermia's father, favors Demetrius and wants him to marry Hermia. Demetrius admitted once that he loved Hermia's friend, Helena, but he later abandoned her. He pursues Hermia even though he knows she does not love him.

Oberon is King of the Fairies. He wants to take revenge on his wife, Titania, Queen of the Fairies, and his method creates confusion and humor in the story.

A MIDSUMMER NIGHT'S DREAM

Once upon a time in Athens, there was a rather strict law regarding the marriage of girls. It had been decided by the Duke that every father had the right to give his daughter's hand in marriage to a man of his choice—and if his daughter were to refuse his offer, then she would be put to death. Now this

law was seldom carried out, as no father wanted to see his daughter killed, but in the case of Egeus and his daughter, Hermia, it was a different story altogether.

Egeus wanted Hermia to marry Demetrius, a noble youth to his liking. However, Hermia knew that Demetrius had formerly professed his love for her dear friend Helena, who was madly in love with him, so she refused to obey her father's orders. Of course, she did not mention that she herself was in love with a handsome man called Lysander.

Theseus, the Duke of Athens, was a noble and kind ruler. He knew that Hermia's decision should be respected, but it was beyond his power to bend the law in her favor. So he gave her an ultimatum—she must either marry Demetrius in four days' time or she would be sent to the gallows.

Hermia now faced a dilemma. She immediately went to Lysander and explained the problem to him. She told him that she only had four days to make up her mind or she would die. Lysander said that one of his aunts lived not too far away, in a place where he knew this law

would not affect Hermia, as its powers were limited to the city of Athens. He asked her to run away with him that night, and told her he would wait for her in the woods outside the city.

Hermia readily agreed to this proposal and went off to make preparations for the escape. But Hermia made one little mistake.

Hermia was a trusting, innocent young girl, so she told her friend Helena about the plan . . . but Helena went and told Demetrius. She knew that Demetrius would follow Hermia

to the woods that night, and she
planned to follow him. Helena
was in love with Demetrius,
and she thought, perhaps, he
would reward her for telling
him of Hermia's plan to flee.

Little did anyone know that the woods were the favorite haunt of tiny magical people known as fairies. Oberon was King of the Fairies and Titania was his queen. They would usually come out at midnight, along with their entourage of little fairies and elves.

However, during Hermia and Lysander's flight, the King and Queen of the Fairies were having a little disagreement. Their arguing had continued for several months, and whenever they started quarrelling, all the little elves would run away and hide out of fear.

17

The cause of the disagreement was that one of Titania's friends, upon her death, had left the Queen of the Fairies with a small child. Oberon now wanted Titania to give

him that little boy as a page,
a request Titania refused.

The night of Hermia's escape,
Titania was walking through the
woods with her maids-in-waiting,
when suddenly Oberon and his

merry band of men came before her. The minute Titania's eyes fell on her husband, she immediately asked her companions to leave. This infuriated Oberon, who said, "Am I not your lord, O rash fairy? Why do you cross me? Give me that little boy as my page."

But Titania merely turned her head away and replied, "Your entire fairy kingdom cannot buy the boy from me." This brought greater anguish to Oberon, who declared that before dawn the next day, she would be begging

21

for his forgiveness. As Titania
left him, Oberon sent for his
favorite counselor, Puck.

Puck was a clever and naughty
sprite who would while away
his time playing pranks in
the neighboring villages. He
would either spoil the milk, or,

using his magical powers, not
allow the cream to be churned
into butter. As if that were
not enough, he would make
people spill ale on themselves,
or would pull chairs out from
under people seated on them.

Oberon asked the mischievous Puck to get him a purple flower called "Love in Idleness," the juice of which was a magic potion—when dropped on the eyelids of a person asleep, it would make them fall in love with the first person they saw upon waking. Oberon knew of another magic potion that would make the charm created by this flower wear off, but he would not tell anyone about this until he had taken the little boy from Titania.

Puck, prankster that he was, was overjoyed at these new orders and rushed off immediately.

While Oberon waited for
his partner in crime to return,
he saw Demetrius walking into
the forest, followed by Helena.
He could see Demetrius trying
to ward off Helena, insulting
her at every opportunity,

but she, unwilling to give
up, kept following him.

Oberon was always friendly
toward true lovers and felt
sorry for poor Helena. So when
Puck returned with the flower,
Oberon ordered him to splash

some of the juice on Demetrius's eyelids if he could catch him asleep. All that Puck needed to remember was to make sure that when Demetrius awoke he saw Helena first. As Puck left to carry out his assignment, Oberon walked off in search of Titania.

Deep in the forest, the fairies were busy singing a lullaby for Titania. Within a few moments, the Queen of the Fairies was fast asleep.

While Oberon was trying to convince Titania to hand over the little boy to him through magic, Hermia and Lysander arrived in the woods. When they were a safe distance from Athens, Hermia declared that she was very tired and wanted to rest for the night. So the two lovers lay down on a bed of moss and were soon fast asleep.

Just then, Puck turned up and concluded that these must be the two people his king had told him about.

Puck poured the juice of
the magical purple flower onto
Lysander's eyelids and left.

No harm would have come of
this if Lysander had seen his love,
Hermia, when he awoke. But
that's not who he saw first . . .

Now, it so happened that
Demetrius, tired of being

 followed
around by
Helena, had
started to run
and was soon
out of her sight.

Walking sadly through
the woods, Helena had come
upon the sleeping pair, Hermia
and Lysander. Overjoyed at
finding them, she nudged
Lysander to wake him up.
And the magic began . . .

The minute he saw Helena,
Lysander began expressing his
love for her. Helena was naturally
shocked to hear him speak
that way. She knew that he was
madly in love with Hermia and

thought he was making fun of her. This made her very upset.

Angry and embarrassed, Helena ran away, tears streaming down her face, while a distraught Lysander was left wondering what had happened. He had obviously forgotten all about

Hermia, who was still fast asleep. By the time Hermia awoke, Lysander was gone. Meanwhile, Demetrius, who was searching the forest for Hermia and Lysander, realized he was lost. Since he was very tired now, he decided to stop for a while and rest. He soon fell asleep.

Oberon, who was passing through the forest at that time, saw Demetrius asleep. Puck had told him about the blunder and, upon finding the original recipient of his scheme, he decided to act himself.

He poured a few drops of the magical juice onto Demetrius's eyelids and left him to sleep.

When Demetrius woke up, lo and behold, the first person he saw was Helena! What a mess this woodland magic had made.

As he started to give the same speech of love that Lysander had made to her before, Lysander arrived in search of Helena. Then they both started to woo the mystified Helena.

Hermia, who was searching the woods for her beloved Lysander, arrived and could not believe what she was seeing. Helena was now convinced that all three of them had decided to make fun of her, and she was seething. Soon, the two women got into a war of words, and the men decided to find a suitable place where they could fight over Helena.

Oberon was completely taken aback by the mixed-up

lovers. He was furious with Puck for messing up the love potion. Puck replied that it was hardly his fault—Oberon had merely asked him to find two lovers, which he had done.

Oberon realized that since he had caused this mess, it was up to him to resolve it. He ordered Puck to create a thick fog over the woods immediately, which would separate the four friends,

causing them each to get lost. He also told Puck to lead the two men away until they became so tired that they would be unable to walk any further and would fall asleep. Then he gave Puck some juice from another plant, which would cause the effects of the purple flower to wear off. Oberon told Puck to drop this potion onto Lysander's eyelids so that when he awoke he would forget all about Helena and go back to Hermia.

While Puck sorted out the mess with the lovers, Oberon left again in search of Titania.

He found her still asleep, so he dropped the magic potion

onto her eyelids, saying, "What you see when you wake, do it for

your true love take." Nearby, he found a clown asleep as well. Through his magic, he replaced

the clown's head with
that of a donkey and woke
him up. As the foolish clown
wandered along, he came across
Titania, who was beginning
to rouse. When she saw
the joker with the donkey's

head, she immediately fell in love with him. Oberon's trick was working!

Titania asked her maids to tend to the man who had completely taken over her heart. The clown, who had no idea

about the donkey's head on his shoulders, was overjoyed at the services he was being offered and decided to sleep again in comfort.

As Titania held his head in her arms and crowned it with flowers, Oberon made his appearance. He bellowed at her, accusing her of taking a donkey for a lover and being unfaithful to him. Titania was ashamed of herself, but there was little she could do. The magic had done its work.

Oberon, playing on Titania's guilt, once again asked for the boy.

Obviously, the Queen of the Fairies was in no position to fight

with her husband. After all, she
had been caught lovingly stroking
a donkey. She immediately sent
for the boy and handed him
over to Oberon as his page.

Now that Oberon had what he
wanted, he immediately reversed

the effects of the magic potion with the help of the other juice. Titania came to her senses, and Oberon told her what he had done. Although Titania was angry initially, she soon relented, and the king and queen were reconciled.

Oberon then told his beloved wife about the lovers. Titania was intrigued, and they set off to find the confused mortals.

The royal fairies saw that Puck had managed to bring all four friends to the same spot without them knowing.

Since they were now asleep,
Puck dropped the new potion
that Oberon had given him
onto Lysander's eyelids.

Hermia was the first to wake
up. She found Lysander sleeping
next to her, and as she was
wondering why he had suddenly

started acting so strangely, he opened his eyes and saw her.

He had now recovered from his bewitched love for Helena, and he stared into Hermia's eyes like he had done so many times before. Hermia told him what had happened to them,

but Lysander could not remember anything. They left together, thinking that it all must have been a dream.

Helena and Demetrius also woke up shortly after. Helena was much calmer after her restful sleep, while Demetrius continued in the same loving tone as before. Helena thought he must be speaking the truth, and as she had always loved him, she was now quite content.

When Helena and Hermia met again later that day, they reconciled their differences and were once again the best of friends. They talked about everything that had happened the night before, but they decided to forget about it, as they had all gotten what they wanted.

Demetrius, now in love with Helena, no longer wanted to marry Hermia, so it was decided that they would all go back to Athens and Demetrius would

inform Egeus of his decision. They held tight to the hope that Hermia's father would repeal the death sentence against her.

Just as they were setting off for Athens, Egeus arrived. He had discovered his daughter had run away and had come to the woods in search of her.

Demetrius told Egeus that he no longer wished to marry Hermia, so Egeus could now allow her to marry Lysander. Egeus declared that they would get married on the fourth day, the day on which Hermia would have been put to death. Demetrius and Helena, now free to love each other, also decided to marry on that very same day.

Oberon and Titania witnessed these events and were overjoyed. Oberon immediately announced a night of revelry throughout the fairy kingdom.